GETTING PAID TO
Work in 3D

DON RAUF

ROSEN
PUBLISHING®

New York

Introduction

Imagine a three-dimensional Roadrunner and Wile E. Coyote appearing on your kitchen table—chasing each other around and around at super-fast speeds. When wearing the latest virtual reality (VR) headset, it's possible to watch 3D versions of these cartoon characters that appear as if they are really in front of you—and you can view them from any angle.

In the movie *The Revenant*, a very real-looking bear appears to be attacking Leonardo DiCaprio. In reality, the effect was accomplished with stuntmen and computer-generated imagery, or CGI. The bear's skeleton, muscles, and skin were all created in layers, and made to move realistically using the principles of 3D animation.

Doctors also use the latest in 3D imaging technology. For example, they can make an exact model of a patient's heart to better understand its structure and how blood flows through it.

The world of 3D graphics is booming. When you see an animated movie today, it's very likely that computer-generated imagery was used to create its 3D characters, objects, and backgrounds.

This technology really took off in 1995, when the first all-CGI movie—*Toy Story*—opened in theaters. The 3D technology swiftly gained in popularity with Pixar Animation Studios, leading the charge with several hit films, including *A Bug's Life*,

Virtual reality headsets have made it possible for people to enter a fully immersive 3D environment. Here, a young woman controls the experience with hand gestures.

Monsters, Inc., Finding Nemo, The Incredibles, Cars, Ratatouille, WALL-E, and *Up*. TV animation also moved toward 3D in the early 2000s, with *Jimmy Neutron* as one of the earliest, most popular examples.

Video games today are driven by 3D animation as well. One of the most recent and exciting advances in 3D animation has been the creation of worlds and characters that can be viewed with virtual reality headsets. These headsets put the viewers in a totally immersive world. Some say that in time, viewers will be able to walk into a 3D-animated movie and actually feel like they're part of the action. Animators who are working with VR technology are also creating hologram characters that appear as if they are moving around in the real world.

If you've always been a fan of animated films and computer games, your interest could translate into a successful career. A 3D-animation or 3D-modeling job combines artistic talent with a certain amount of technical smarts, so it can be rewarding on two levels. Plus, the way the technology is being used is expanding rapidly, so the possibilities are exciting and continually growing.

Chapter ONE

Step into the 3D World

You're running through a castle, waving a sword. You're attempting to save a princess from a castle dungeon. You are battling a treacherous wizard. You are driving a racecar through a post-apocalyptic city. You are battling aliens in outer space. You are Batman fighting villains in Gotham City. You are running, swimming, and flying in fictional worlds that all seem realistic because they are presented in 3D in popular video games. *Halo, Batman, Avatar, Jurassic Park*, and many other games are presented in a three-dimensional universe. Many animated movies and TV shows also plunge you into a 3D world.

Computer-generated imagery (CGI) has brought more depth and a more realistic quality to fictional worlds and characters. The objects look like things you can wrap your hands around. This is opposed to 2D animation, which is flat. Images in two dimensions do not pop like in 3D. And with today's technology, 3D has become even more 3D. When movies and games created in 3D are watched through special goggles or headsets, the

Many of today's hit movies, including *Avatar, Toy Story 3,* and *The Avengers,* are made in 3D. They are viewed by wearing special glasses.

objects and characters can look like they are literally jumping off the screen.

New virtual-reality technology takes 3D a step further by making users feel like they are literally moving their bodies through a virtual world, one that appears to be real. Of course, nothing beats real life when it comes to 3D, but computer scientists have been working toward the goal of simulating real life as translated through digital technology.

THE BIRTH OF 3D

The rise of 3D has been so rapid that it's almost hard to imagine that the world of animation was predominantly 2D before the early 1970s. The first known projected animation goes all the way back to 1877, when the French science teacher Charles-Émile Reynaud invented the optical toy, called the Praxinoscope. As a cylinder with twelve frames of animation spins, stationary

Early animation came in the form of flip books, which were very popular in the latter part of the 1800s. The filoscope, pictured here, contained one hundred or so frames.

mirrors in the center of the Praxinoscope showed a single moving image. In the latter half of the 1800s, the public became further intrigued with the world of animation when flip books were mass-produced and distributed.

One of the first standard film animations was *The Enchanted Drawing*, made in 1900. It's unique in that the drawn items interact with a live actor. So as early as the turn of the twentieth century, people were trying to think of innovative ways to use animation and make it seem like it was more a part of the real world.

Over the next few decades, 2D animation made great strides. Walt Disney was one of the pioneers. In 1928, he produced the Mickey Mouse movie short *Steamboat Willie,* which was one of the earliest cartoons to have voice, music, and sound effects printed onto the film itself.

Around 1933, an animator at Disney Studios is said to have invented the storyboarding process—using still pictures to plan the plot of movie. The process is still used today to create films and video games. Disney was also an early force in movie animation, by taking the art form from black and white to color.

In 1937, Disney made another major leap in animation when he released the eighty-three-minute-long *Snow White and the Seven Dwarfs*. It is one of the earliest and most famous full-length animated features. When he released the movie, Disney was in financial jeopardy and his company was on the verge of bankruptcy. He invested four years and $1.5 million in the project. Fortunately, it was a huge hit and earned more than $184 million over time.

Disney became a celebrated filmmaker. His successes just kept coming after that, and his fortunes skyrocketed. From the 1930s to 1950s, animation boomed. Color TV in the 1950s brought a flood of color cartoons into the homes of America.

One of the earliest animated films was *Gertie the Dinosaur,* a twelve-minute movie by Winsor McCay released in 1914. McCay was also the creator of the comic strip *Little Nemo.*

EARLY 3D ANIMATION

As traditional animation developed, so did a form of 3D animation called stop-motion. Stop-motion brought a noncomputerized version of 3D to audiences. With the stop-motion technique, objects are filmed in a series of slightly different positions, so it makes the objects appear to move. The first stop-motion animation is said to have been a short film from 1898 called *The Humpty Dumpty Circus,* in which toy animals and acrobats come to life.

A Quick Exploration of 3D Animation

While you might be familiar with 3D animation from movies and games, a few websites let you explore the capabilities of this technology. Here are a few worth taking a peek at online.

Mixamo. This site lets you animate a 3D character with absolutely no knowledge of 3D technology. You create the 3D model according to your specification and get it moving according to your directions.

Sketchfab. Sketchfab calls itself the place to be for 3D. People who make 3D animations and characters share their work. It's a great way to quickly view a wide variety of creations.

ABCya! Animate. This site lets the user easily create an animation online. It provides a tutorial that makes it simple for anyone to get started.

One of the earliest and most famous examples of stop-motion that lives on to this day is King Kong. The giant 3D ape was brought to life through stop-motion and 3D modeling. Ray Harryhausen showed the potential of the technique by creating mythical creatures in movies in the 1960s and '70s, such as *Jason and the Argonauts* and *The Golden Voyage of Sinbad.*

Many people today are still familiar with Gumby, an animated clay figure born in the 1950s, and the Christmas classic *Rudolph the Red-Nosed Reindeer*, which was produced in 1964. Although computer technology would eventually be used to create 3D, these more primitive stop-motion productions continue to be popular with audiences.

Current animators still use the stop-motion technique. Aardman Studios, for example, found great success with *Wallace and Gromit*, first introduced in 1990. Recently, the hit movie *The Boxtrolls* was filmed using stop animation, as was the film *Shaun the Sheep*. So while computer technology has made 3D animation faster, there is still an appeal and an audience for this older technique.

Note that while these are examples of creating 3D animation, there was also a form of 3D film-making called 3D stereoscopy. With this technique, two slightly offset images are captured and create the illusion of 3D.

Stereoscopic photography goes back to the 1800s. In 1953, the first color 3D film opened—*The House of Wax* starring Vincent Price. Moviegoers watched it wearing special stereoscopic glasses.

THE COMPUTER 3D WORLD

Drawing pictures for animation is an incredibly time-consuming process. A feature film generally requires twenty-four frames per

second, so hand drawing can require an incredible amount of time and labor to complete. According to publicity material, *Snow White* required at least 570 crewmembers. Most of them were animators and watercolor artists.

Experiments in computer graphics began in the 1940s and 1950s. Between 1961 and 1963, MIT student Ivan Sutherland created a drawing program called Sketchpad. It allowed a person to draw simple shapes on a computer screen, and the computer could adjust the lines drawn according to a set of rules input in the computer. In the 1960s, the auto industry developed its own programs for making sophisticated drawings in the computer.

In the 1970s, computer scientists figured out how to make the drawings three-dimensional. In 1972, Ed Catmull (a cofounder of the animation studio

Steve Jobs (*center*), the chief executive officer of Apple, helped build Pixar Animation Studios with cofounders Ed Catmull (*left*) and John Lasseter.

Pixar) and Fred Parke created what many people consider the world's first 3D digitally rendered movie. It was an animated version of Catmull's left hand. The new techniques they developed were the basis for 3D rendering used today in animation, video games, and special effects.

Rendering is the process of converting 3D wire-frame models into images in the computer. The images look like they have three dimensions. A wire-frame model is a presentation of points and lines that define either the edges or center lines of a physical object. With the right software, a computer animator today adds shading, color, and surfaces to the wire-frame object that he or she constructed. When the object is rendered and ready, an animator can put the 3D image into motion.

For Catmull and Parke to do this, they made a real-life physical model of Ed's hand. Then they drew polygons in ink all over the surface of the model. The model and the shapes were then digitized. The data created were lines that made polygons in the computer. The polygons served as the building blocks, which could be positioned to create a very elaborate computer model of the hand.

With this wire-frame structure in place, the computer scientists then covered the hand in different types of shading using computer software. Through a 3D animation program that Catmull wrote, the hand and its fingers could be manipulated on screen, just as a human hand could be moved with most of that range of motion. It could be viewed from every different angle— from above, below, and the side. Using this technique, they also created an early 3D model of a moveable human face, which could be manipulated.

A LEAP INTO FILMS

In 1976, *Futureworld*, about a futurist theme park, became the first feature film to use 3D computer-generated imagery. *Star Wars* followed in 1977, introducing viewers to some wire-frame imagery in scenes with the Death Star and Millennium Falcon spacecraft. Other 3D highlights in film included fifteen minutes of fully rendered CGI in *Tron* in 1982, and the first water CGI effect in *The Abyss* in 1989.

By the 1990s, CGI effects were photorealistic, as seen in *The Terminator* and *Jurassic Park*. In the world of animation, *Toy Story*, created by Pixar, became the first fully CGI animated feature film in 1995. Pixar perfected effects in 3D such as flexible characters,

The advanced 3D imagery in *The Matrix* reached a whole new level of sophistication and introduced audiences to new 360-degree visuals and a slow-motion effect called "bullet time."

hand-painted textures, and motion blur. The company went on to release animated hits such as *A Bug's Life, Monsters, Inc., Finding Nemo, The Incredibles, Ratatouille, WALL-E,* and *Up.*

In 1999, *The Matrix* showed advances in 3D effects. Using an effect called bullet time, bullets shot at the hero appeared to freeze or slow dramatically. As the bullets stopped or made a slow advance in the air, the camera appeared to move around the action in a circular motion at normal speed. In the meantime, the hero bent his body to evade the path of the bullets.

In the gaming world, the PlayStation and Nintendo 64 consoles presented 3D platforms. In time, games such as *Grand Theft Auto* and *Crysis* showed how detailed and vast a 3D universe could be in a video game. The game *Minecraft* introduced players to a unique 3D world that they could build and alter according to their own imaginations.

In movies, the use of 3D effects combined with real actors advanced to new levels. *Avatar* and *The Lord of the Rings* trilogy showed the possibilities. Using a real actor and the latest motion-capture technology, *Lord of the Rings* director Peter Jackson and his team were able to develop the character Gollum. Gollum had very natural motions because he was created combining CGI with a live actor.

Today, 3D modeling and animation are used outside of the entertainment industry in architecture, product design, medicine, and military training. The technology is rapidly expanding into a number of different fields.

Chapter TWO

Get on Course: Education Matters

Though you may enjoy 3D animation, you need to develop skills in both art and computer technology if you want to get paid to work in this field. The best way to get started is by focusing on developing your artistic talent. Making anything in 3D requires a visual sense, so creating art on a regular basis can help. Practice makes perfect, as the old saying goes, so always engage in drawing, painting, sketching, modeling with clay, or other visual art endeavors. The more you create, the better you will get. You don't necessarily have to be an artistic genius to get started in the field, but some skills in drawing especially can help.

A foundation of traditional art courses, such as drawing and sculpting, can help a student develop the skills needed to create interesting 3D animation.

In 2D animation, artistic skills were more of a necessity because the animator had to draw a series of frames to create the sense of movement. Using computer technology in 3D, you can move your characters with software to animate them. To understand animation at its most basic level, you might want to get a pad of paper and make a flip book with simple animation. Try drawing a simple stick figure and, in a series of drawings, show how it would move. As each slightly changed image flips by, the stick figure appears to be in motion. This fundamental principle applies in the more sophisticated realm of 3D animation as well.

Also, check what art classes your school may offer. Serious training in art can only help as you bring your 3D visions to life. Look for extracurricular opportunities at your school as well. Drawing a comic strip for your school newspaper, for example, can teach the story writing skills of character development and continuity. Making a comic strip is also closely related to making storyboards, which are essential to plotting scenes in a movie or game.

STORYTELLING IS KING

A lot of 3D work involves character development and storytelling. Characters you create in 3D are sort of like actors. They have to convey emotions such as joy, anger, jealousy, and fear, to name a few. They have to interact with other 3D characters and move in a natural way.

To get an idea about how to convey human emotions, you can benefit from taking acting classes or participating in a school play.

Animators often depict a range of emotions and actions. They may benefit from acting classes, which show how to use the body to express different feelings and movements.

Acting is a great way to figure out how to convey different emotions and reactions. Acting gives a sense of how the human body moves when interacting with others. Also, check if your school offers film and video production classes. These courses not only help understand filmed action and acting, they may even offer a chance to work with 3D animation and modeling, if the school is equipped with advanced computer equipment and software.

Plays, movies, and videos all involve storytelling skills as well. The story drives any successful 3D animated feature. English, literature, and writing classes can help you become a better writer. Plus, the more stories and novels you read, the more ideas you will get for plots, characters, and settings.

GETTING TECHNICAL

Those who want to get paid to work in 3D need more than just artistic skills. The field also requires technical skill. Computer animation software today allows the user to do amazing things with relative ease and speed. This software enables a person to create a sophisticated lighting setup without lights, a crowd in a stadium without hiring extras, and elaborate costumes and makeup without making the clothes or applying real makeup, lipstick, and eyeliner.

Computer coding makes the world of 3D animation possible. Coding is writing the instructions that tell the computer what to do. It relies on algorithms, which are mathematical formulas.

Code is the language behind animation software. With the right software, animators can make almost any action happen on screen—from exploding cars to rainstorms to chase scenes and more. Your school may have computer classes or an extracurricular computer club that offers lessons in using this software. But any experience using software and creating code can help.

Code is written using computer languages. One of the most popular computer languages is JavaScript, but other top computer languages include PHP, Python, Ruby, Perl, SQL (pronounced sequel), Swift, and C, C++, and C# (C Sharp).

Computer animation today depends on advanced programming and software. Learning some fundamentals about how to code can be useful in this field.

Many computer animators don't write code, but those with some coding knowledge have a better grasp on the software tools they are using. The 3D animators who understand code may be able to use that knowledge to produce their own 3D software or make improvements on existing software.

Many websites today provide free courses in coding. Codecademy offers no-charge interactive training in nine computer languages. MIT has free open courseware, including an "Introduction to Programming in Java" and "Introduction to Computer Science and Programming." Khan Academy offers many coding classes, including "Intro to JavaScript: Drawing &

Animation." Scratch is a free programming language developed by MIT that allows you to create your own interactive stories, games, and animations. People who create their animations then can post and share their masterpieces on the Scratch website.

SOFTWARE THAT MAKES THE MAGIC

Flash is another great animation software. Although Flash has traditionally been for 2D animation, the software has added 3D capabilities. It's a fun software to experiment with, and it doesn't take days and days to come up with a cool animation. To get started, check out one of the many tutorials online. For example, Lynda.com offers an introduction to Flash, as does TheVirtualInstructor.com.

Maya (or Autodesk Maya) is a very popular 3D computer graphics software that can run on the Windows, OS X, or Linux operating systems. It allows for 3D modeling, animation, and simulation. The software has been used in the movies *Avatar, Finding Nemo, Up, Monsters, Inc., Hugo, Rango,* and *Frozen.* TV shows such as *The Walking Dead, Bones,* and *Once Upon a Time* have also relied on this technology to make special effects. The Maya website provides a free trial and has its own learning channel, so you can experiment with it. 3D by Buzz is a free outlet for beginners. Also, look into Creative Applications Network and Digital Arts Guild for more lessons at no charge.

Another hugely popular 3D software is Blender, and it's totally free and open source (meaning the original source code is made freely available and may be redistributed and modified). Blender is used to create animated films, visual effects, art, printed models, interactive applications, and video games. It has attracted a large and enthusiastic online community, which is

A student in a computer graphics class creates a digital image with Maya, software commonly used to produce 3D animation and modeling.

always ready to offer help. Visit Blender.org to learn more. Other software to look into include 3ds Max, Cinema 4D, RealFlow, NUKE, RenderMan, Mental Ray, Houdini, and Poser.

While you can take some free courses online, you might also want to look into a few for-pay sessions. The online animation school Animation Apprentice teaches the art of 3D character and creature animation in a thirty-week course. Also check out Animation Mentor and AnimSchool.

Kenny Roy, the author of *Sams Teach Yourself Maya in 24 Hours*, gives a few tips for those trying to master 3D animation

A Turn for the Better Through Interning

An internship through a school can help a student build needed skills while earning college credit. While many internships do not offer payment, some provide interns with a stipend.

The experience from an internship helps build a résumé and can give a beginner connections to land that first job. When looking for an internship, think what this experience can teach you. An internship can give you an opportunity to work alongside some of the best in the business and prove that you're a committed hard worker. Pixar, for example, has a very competitive internship program.

To land a good internship in this field, a demo reel with examples of your work is usually required. In an interview with CreativeBloq, Andrew Gordon, directing animator at Pixar, said that it's important to stick out from the pack: "You get a lot of reels that are the same type of reel all featuring the same exercises. But the ones that are rare are where the applicant has done something different in their approach."

Companies such as Pixelhunters (which makes high-quality visual effects and 3D artwork), Sony Pictures, EA, and Blizzard Entertainment all provide internships that involve developing 3D elements. One production company advertised for an intern who had experience with Autodesk Maya, which is computer animation and modeling software. The company also wanted a candidate with strength in hard surface and organic modeling. Hard surface modeling is used to make 3D images of either machined or man-made objects, while organic modeling is for things in the natural world—trees, a dog, etc. Sculpting skills were a plus—sculpting in 3D modeling means using digital tools that allow you to push and pull and reshape the interconnected surface mesh of polygons that make up a 3D object. Having animation experience was a bonus for this job but not mandatory. The company also sought someone with excellent interpersonal communication skills, as well as a good attitude in a collaborative studio. Interns were expected to work closely with the computer graphics supervisor to hone their 3D talents in a production environment.

and modeling. He says to journal your progress, establish a network of like-minded artists, get and give feedback on work, set a schedule to create, remove distractions, create a workspace, and find a mentor.

THE COLLEGE ADVANTAGE

High school classes, online training, and self-taught lessons can only go so far in this field. Most professionals get a college education to build skills and make job connections.

In college, students develop skills in fine arts, graphic arts, computer animation, graphic and photo imaging software, as well as 3D animation software. Completing a degree shows that a person has the technical proficiency to succeed in this

To truly master the techniques of 3D animation, a person may pursue a degree in this field at a major college or university, such as the Rhode Island School of Design.

occupation. As students work toward graduation, they need to steadily build a portfolio. A portfolio features examples of the budding artist's best work and includes demonstrations of technical proficiency with different software and technology.

Scores of colleges and universities offer four-year and two-year degrees in computer animation. Animation majors at Carnegie Mellon University in Pittsburgh, Pennsylvania, can take courses in game design, animation technology and art, and artificial intelligence development.

CalArts, founded by Walt Disney Productions, has several top-rated 3D animation programs. Other well-respected schools that concentrate on this field include The Art Institute of Boston, College of Art and Design–Lesley University, Brigham Young University, Pratt Institute, Ringling College of Art and Design, Rhode Island School of Design, Rochester Institute of Technology, Savannah College of Art and Design, University of Central Florida, and University of Southern California.

Some of the more innovative programs in 3D technology include the game technology program at University of California, Irvine, which teaches how to construct multimodal role-playing games that integrate 3D graphics with the internet. Virginia Polytechnic and State University has a 3D Interaction Laboratory that explores "immersive virtual environments."

College is a perfect place to get hands-on training, and it's this type of experience that typically counts most in the real world. Keeping up to speed on the latest advances in technology is essential to competing in this swiftly evolving field. The most important thing you should have when you graduate is an online portfolio and a solid demo reel.

Chapter THREE

Take Your Skills to a New Dimension

Professionals in 3D animation have to master a unique set of skills that combine creative and technical worlds. This is a constantly evolving field, in which the technology keeps advancing with new software tools. The computer programs can take some time to learn, but these devices can make the impossible possible and save time and money. A lot of the time-consuming steps that regular animation requires can now be done in far less time via a computer.

COMPUTER MODELS

Coming up with characters is one of the earliest steps in 3D animation. Before an artist builds the character in 3D, he or she will make model sheets showing the character from different angles and making different expressions in a stage called preproduction. Once a design for an object or character is decided, the first step in is to create it in 3D and make a "model" in the computer.

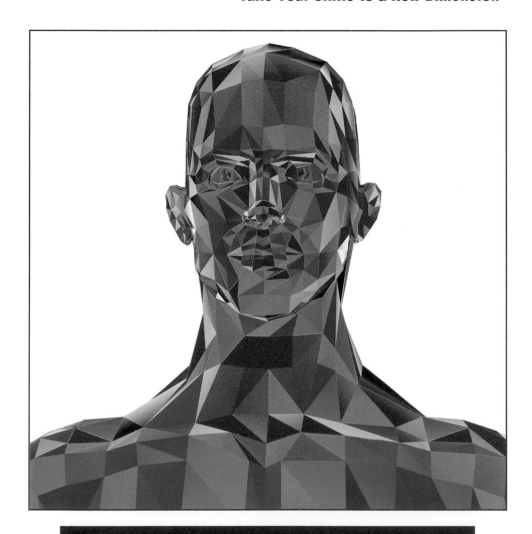

Many 3D models are constructed from polygons, which are placed to depict the surface and structure of a character or object. Artists manipulate the polygons to get a desired look.

The model is often constructed of polygons, which represent the surfaces of the object. The collection of vertices, edges, and faces that form the 3D object is called a polygon mesh. A main character in a 3D animated movie can have ten thousand to thirty thousand polygons. This is called the polycount. The higher the polycount, the longer it takes a computer to render the image.

Other Approaches to 3D Modeling

Polygonal modeling is the most common 3D modeling type, and it is very flexible to work with. If you pursue the career further, investigate other modeling approaches. For example, NURBS, which stands for non-uniform rational b-spline, is a method to produce very smooth curves and surfaces.

NURBS is commonly used in computer-aided design (CAD). CAD software is used by architects, engineers, drafters, artists, and others to create precision drawings or technical illustrations that can be in 2D or 3D. Also, there is digital sculpting, which is a process that takes a low detail or no-details computer model and lets you manipulate it as if it were clay— refining details until you have a detailed form.

THE RENDERING PROCESS

Three-dimensional rendering is actually the producing of the image, or viewable result, based on all the data input. (A render can also be a series of these images.) The rendering process results in a three-dimensional image of an object, character, or scene based on the information input. The rendering creates a picture from a specific location from a specific angle. Through

Sully, the big blue lovable star of *Monsters, Inc.,* shows how advanced and detailed 3D special effects have become. His fur is made of 5.5 million animated hairs.

rendering, realistic effects can be added to the visuals—lighting, shadows, color, texture, and special optical effects.

Rendering can take hours depending on how complex the image is and how much information is being translated. In effect, the computer has to take a "photograph" of every pixel in the 3D model. A pixel is a minute area of illumination on a display screen. An image can consist of millions of pixels.

Pixar has about 114,000 frames in one of its feature films. This requires 800,000 machine hours to render about two to fifteen hours per frame. It took about twenty-nine hours to render a single frame of *Monsters University*, according to supervising technical director Sanjay Bakshi. After all, Sully, the big loveable blue monster, had 5.5 million individual hairs in his fur—and that kind of detail takes time.

This movie was also a breakthrough because the tech pros came up with a realistic system of lighting called "global illumination." Through this technology, lighting sources, such as the sun, were accurately simulated to produce very real-looking light and shadows. 3D technology has also brought many animated special effects to life—explosions, fires, floods, and dust storms can all be simulated.

REAL-TIME RENDERING: A GAMING ESSENTIAL

A 3D computer game relies on a process called *real-time rendering*. Because a game player is deciding what a character on screen should do in real time, the game character has to be rendered superfast as the player moves it along on screen.

With real-time rendering, frames are loaded instantaneously to create images that simulate actual movement. The video game loads images so fast that the motion seems fluid.

This real-time technology enables interactivity. The level of details and visual quality is far less in a video game, so it can render much faster. Compared to a 3D game character, a Pixar character, for example, will have much more geometry, texture, surfacing, and lighting. Reducing the complexity increases the rendering speed.

DETAILING AND SCULPTING A 3D MODEL

Different aspects of your 3D model will add to its complexity and polycount. For example, if a model's silhouette is complicated, that requires more information. As you learn more about rendering, you will find that triangulating your polygons will make rendering faster. A 3D animator may also make several models of the same character with different levels of detail (LOD). If a character is farther away in the distance from the camera, that character appears smaller and requires less detail.

Artists can shape their characters and objects using 3D sculpting tools, such as ZBrush (*pictured here*), Mudbox, and Cinema 4D.

Software has made it easier to reshape a 3D model. Through 3D sculpting tools, artists can push, pull, smooth, stretch, grab, or pinch the digital object, almost as if shaping it like virtual modeling clay. Several sculpting programs are on the market, including ZBrush, Mudbox, and Cinema 4D.

The entire skeleton of a character is especially important in films and games. If constructed right, the skeleton lets the character move smoothly and naturally. Building this virtual skeleton is called rigging. The model applied to the skeleton is sometimes called the mesh, and the skin is projected over the mesh.

The character Gollum in *The Lord of the Rings* came to life on screen through motion capture, which applied the movements and expressions of a real actor to a 3D character.

Some people describe the model as the glove placed over the hand. The animator assigns different parts of the skeleton a variable called an avar. Every part of the character that needs to move is assigned an avar. Assigning an avar to a figure's arm lets the animator move it in different directions by altering the value. The character Woody in *Toy Story* has 712 avars—212 of those were in his face so he could show a subtle range of emotion. Developed in 1976, the Facial Action Coding System (FACS) is an anatomically based system for comprehensively describing all observable facial movement. Animators refer to FACS to help establish different facial movements.

Often, rigging will involve figuring out the clothes for a character as well, and how these garments will have to move naturally. So while an animated production might not have a costume designer, it might have a rigger who creates the 3D costumes.

As the animator changes different values for the avars, he or she creates motion from frame to frame. Through a technology called motion capture (or *mocap* for short), lights or markers are placed on a real person who acts out the part. These sensors track real-life motions, which can be translated to a computer model. A great example of motion capture is in *The Lord of the Rings* movie. The actor Andy Serkis was filmed wearing many sensors on his body. In this way, the Gollum character could be built around his motions, expressions, and overall presence.

WHAT'S ON THE SURFACE?

Once a basic model is completed, a 3D artist will turn to texturing, shading, and coloring. Adding detail, surface texting, or color to a 3D model is called texture mapping. The process can be compared to wrapping a plain box with wrapping paper. Color mapping, sometimes called diffuse mapping, defines the color of your surface polygons.

Bump mapping provides details that make the 3D object look like it has raised or lowered details. Other mapping techniques that affect how the surface of your object looks are displacement mapping and parallax mapping. Specularity mapping is a technique that adds specularity or "shininess" to your object. Alpha mapping makes parts of an object more transparent.

When you need a larger overall background, there is a technique called tiling. With tiling, you can take a small patch of texture and repeat it in a grid. For example, you could easily repeat a brick wall over an extended area. Decals are extra effects—such as bullet holes—that can be added to walls or objects. A shader is a set of instructions applied to a 3D model that lets the computer know how the model should be displayed and includes all the information on shading, texturing, and coloring. Different software makes it possible for animators to show subtle textures. In *Monsters University*, the monster students rub a statue for good luck. Sophisticated technology provided the means to create a spot on that statue that looked realistically worn and shiny.

WHEN TOO REAL IS NOT GOOD

Those involved in animation technology have strived to make 3D characters more and more realistic. But an odd thing happened in their pursuit of realism. Animators found that if their virtual character became too real, audiences did not like it. They called the phenomenon the "uncanny valley." When a simulated human reached a level of realism that was too true, people were uncomfortable or even repulsed. Animators

How "Soft Skills" Can Make a Difference

Hard skills are the practical talents a person needs to perform a specific job. Soft skills are a little more subtle but no less important. These are interpersonal skills and character traits that a young worker can hone in almost any job.

Businesses appreciate these soft skills, and they often go a long way to career success. Here are twenty common soft skills from which 3D animators and modelers can benefit:

- Teamwork
- Communication
- Critical thinking
- Negotiation
- Storytelling
- Leadership
- Interpersonal skills
- Adaptability
- Management skills
- Strong work ethic
- Timeliness
- Neatness and organization
- Dependability
- Problem-solving
- Coaching coworkers
- Fitting with corporate culture
- Going the extra mile
- Flexibility
- Suggesting improvements/ accepting feedback
- Taking initiative

today are aware of this and strive to avoid descending into the uncanny valley.

In addition to characters and objects, computer animators also conjure up vast landscapes, backgrounds, settings, and buildings. This can be much more involved for those who are making video games because game designers build worlds where characters can travel wherever they want to go. Film and television creators only make worlds that they want the audience to see.

SETTING CHARACTERS IN MOTION

Creating 3D characters, objects, and sets is a major process. The next step is to get the creations moving across the screen. To plot the motion in an animated film or video game, professionals use a technique called keyframing. This is making drawings that define the starting and endpoints of an animated sequence.

A keyframe is a single image in that sequence. Each keyframe is a significant moment or a pivotal point in the motion. Imagine animating a batter swinging. The keyframes may be the bat poised to swing and the bat completing the swing. With these major points of action marked, animators go back and do the inbetweening, or tweening. This means making the images between the key frames.

In digital animation, thirty frames per second is the average, so having the aid of a computer saves time. (Note that animators have found that rates higher than 75–120 frames/second make no improvement in realism or smoothness because of how the eye and brain process images.) At times in the working world, the senior animators may do the keyframes and the junior animators may take care of the tweening. Sometimes, computer software

Making 3D animated faces move to match actors' voices can be especially challenging. Here, an artist has constructed a model of Dylan Thomas, which recites one of his poems.

can fill the keyframes as directed. But make no mistake: You don't just push a button and tell the computer to animate. You use the computer software as a tool, which makes the job easier.

A challenge for many animators is to create facial and mouth movements that match the recorded voices in the script.

Animators listen to recorded tracks and sync character mouth shapes to the spoken words. Actors are often videotaped while they deliver their lines so the animators have a visual reference. As mentioned earlier, motion capture may be used to simulate realistic behavior and actions with animated characters. In some cases, the animation is done first and the voice actors match the on-screen mouth motions, but the opposite approach adds more realism.

The last step in a production of film, show, or video is called postproduction. This involves the editing of the final footage, inserting any final effects, making any sound fixes, and taking care of any other needed adjustments. When the final check is complete, the 3D product is ready for the world to see.

Chapter FOUR

Find a Job or Make Your Own

Once a potential 3D animator has learned the required skills and gotten educational training, he or she can start the job hunt. While many opportunities are in animation, special effects, and game design, there are other areas that use 3D technology that might match your personal interests.

Three-dimensional modelers work for advertising firms, graphic design studios, web designers, architects, medical and science companies, colleges and universities, manufacturers, aerospace firms, environmental agencies, the automotive industry, major retailers, crime labs, interior designers, real estate companies, and toy makers.

This job requires highly specialized skills, so there is a demand for 3D modelers in many industries. Even the fashion industry hires 3D pros who can make designs into models on the computer screen. These models can be easily adjusted in different ways—viewed in varying lengths and colors.

Three-dimensional modelers apply their skills in a range of fields. They can even be used in forensics to reconstruct a person's face based on his or her skull.

Also, a museum of natural history may need the service of a 3D modeler for forensic facial reconstruction. In 2004, a scientist and an artist at the University of Western Ontario collaborated on the computerized facial reconstruction of a 2,200-year-old mummy. Using scans of the skull, the artist would create a 3D model of what the mummy must have looked like in real-life ages ago.

Check out the Bureau of Labor Statistics (BLS) website for the most current salaries of multimedia artists such as 3D animators. Those in the top of their field can earn well. The BLS also expects opportunities to grow. Many 3D modelers work project-to-project as freelancers. Sometimes working freelance is a good way to explore opportunities, and these can lead to possible full-time employment.

THE ONLINE SEARCH

Major job search sites, such as Indeed.com, Simply Hired, Monster.com, CareerBuilder, and US.jobs, list employment opportunities for animators and modelers. Upwork and Freelancer. com feature freelance gigs. For sites dedicated to animation work, the Animation World Network has a career connection section that provides leads on employment opportunities, and Animation Boss is bursting with job possibilities.

Other sites dedicated to the tech industry are worth checking, such as Dice.com. The 3D pro may also want to sign up with staffing organizations that can connect them to opportunities, such as Robert Half Technology, TheLadders, and Harvey Nash.

Other online sites, like Craigslist, are not limited to job listings but still advertise job openings. Craigslist is increasingly being used by major employers to find potential hires. This is a huge, mostly free classified ad site (meaning that the ads are arranged by categories or "classes") organized by locations. Take warning and use caution using Craigslist, however—scammers sometimes try to gain personal information from visitors to the site. Use good judgment and make sure an ad you respond to is legitimate. The website Mashable, which is a source for tech, digital cultural, and entertainment content, also has a job board dedicated to digital and tech jobs.

Some employment experts say that 80 percent of jobs are found through networking, and social media has made the networking much easier. LinkedIn is a networking site specifically designed for job seekers who post their profiles on the site, sharing their professional background and qualifications. The site not only helps people make professional connections, it also features job postings.

Other social media sites such as Facebook and Twitter can help job seekers broadcast to all their connections that they are looking for work. Spreading the word is often the key to landing that perfect employment opportunity.

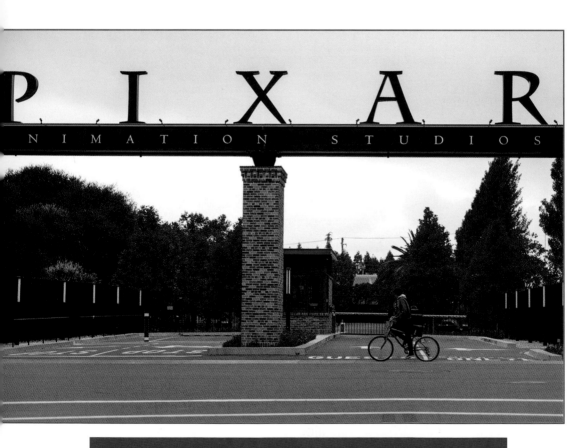

Top employers in this field include Pixar, Walt Disney Animation Studios, DreamWorks Animation, Studio Ghibli, Cartoon Network, Nickelodeon, Lucasfilm, and EA, to name just a few.

Job seekers might also target businesses that interest them, such as some of the big players in the industry (Pixar, Disney, and DreamWorks in entertainment, or Nintendo, Electronic Arts, and Activision in the gaming world).

THE IN-PERSON SEARCH

Job fairs and conferences are also terrific networking experiences. These events bring together many employers. They can be an ideal way to explore job options and make your talents known. Also, attend film festivals and consider volunteering with a related professional organization, such as ASIFA-Hollywood/The International Animated Film Society or the Animation Guild. These professional groups also provide leads on job opportunities and possible connections to mentors. A mentor is a seasoned pro who is willing to help guide and advise how to forge a career path.

Animation Career Review wrote that the following cities are particularly good locations for those who want to get paid to create works in three dimensions: San Francisco, New York City, Toronto, Vancouver, Los Angeles, Seattle, Chicago, Portland, Boston, and Greenwich, Connecticut. (Greenwich may be unexpected—it is not only home to hedge funds and financial services; the major computer animation studio Blue Sky is located here. The company is dedicated to creating high-end character animation and visual effects for the commercial and feature-film industries. Other entertainment and game-related firms have offices there as well.)

Those who are very skilled at 3D can work from almost anywhere in the world, doing all their business via the internet. If you become super experienced in the field, you might consider

opening your own 3D modeling or animation business. Starting your own business takes a big commitment of time and energy to get clients and meet their needs. Those who take the plunge into starting their own operation must define their business, write a business plan, find funding, get customers, and always look for new ways to grow.

Some firms specifically create 3D models for other businesses, and some sites allow those who make 3D models to post and sell their work. These sites include TurboSquid, CGTrader, and 3DExport. The 3D artists who advertise their 3D creations on these sites can earn some extra income, selling to organizations or individuals that need premade content.

To keep up with advances in 3D animation, enthusiasts may attend conventions, fairs, and expos. Here, an attendee checks out the 3D Print Studio at Walt Disney Company's D23 Expo.

How 3D Animators Got Their Start

Recently, at the computer animation conference Siggraph (Special Interest Group on Graphics and Interactive Techniques), top 3D animators gathered together to share their thoughts on how they got into the business and what helped them. Here are a few tips they gave:

Peter Docter, who worked directing *Up, Monsters, Inc.,* and *Inside Out*, attended the California Institute of the Arts. He said that he originally thought learning to draw was the most important thing, but he left school thinking that acting and storytelling were more vital skills to learn. He looks for material that really shows the character of its creator.

Mike Mitchell, director of *Shrek Forever After* and contributor to *Shrek the Third* and *Kung Fu Panda*, said he started "in lonely nerddom." He was drawing at age five and got his first movie camera at age nine. He got involved with animation while attending California Institute of the Arts. He said, "Who knew animation would be as big as it is now? Computer-generated imagery (CGI) is a new tool that expands its scope. That is evolving every month." His advice to budding 3D artists is to follow your personal vision and make the film of your choice.

Kirk Wise, creator of *Open Season,* said he got infatuated with animation by watching Saturday morning cartoons.

He was inspired early on to make his own comic books and then went to California Institute of the Arts, where he made animated films. Wise tells young 3D animators to read widely because it "refills your creative batteries."

TYPES OF JOBS

The opportunities in 3D fall under different titles. Listings may call for an animator, character modeler, or a concept artist. For a compositor position, an individual needs to know how to construct a final image by combining layers of previously created material, including rendered computer animation, special effects, graphics, 2D animation, live action, and static background plates. Some careers are specifically for 3D renderers. Renderers may find work in construction, product manufacturing, architecture, engineering, marketing, or entertainment. In the film industry, you might find a niche in applying 3D modeling to make special effects for live-action productions.

An example of want ads in animation might announce that a company is looking for someone with a strong understanding of traditional animation principles and how they can be used to establish character personality. Text for an ad might read: "We seek a self-motivated, excellent communicator, and a great team-player attitude. Able to work creatively and effectively with team members of various disciplines. Proven problem-solving and model-making ability. Skill in one or more related disciplines—illustration, modeling, rigging or technical art. TV or film animation experience helpful."

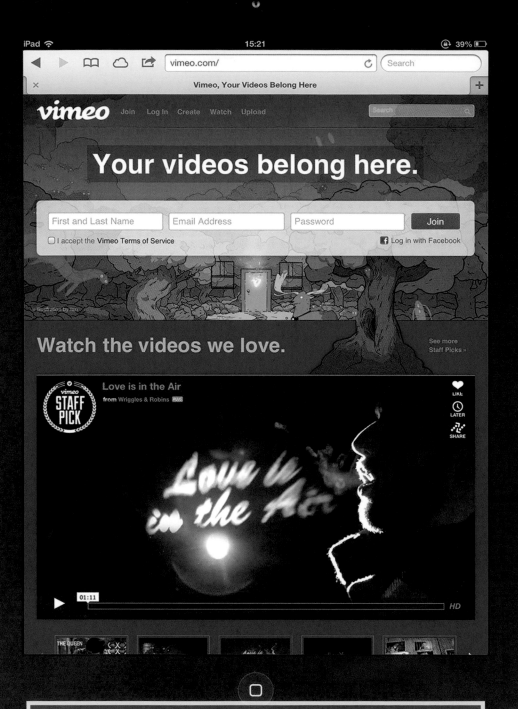

To get a foot in the door of a 3D animation studio, a job seeker needs samples of work, such as videos showing off the artist's talents.

GENERAL TOOLS FOR JOB HUNTING

No matter what job you pursue, some universal tools are required for the hunting process. The résumé is the main thing every job seeker must have. A résumé is a summary of your skills, abilities, and accomplishments, including educational background. The résumé has to be error-free and well written.

Most animators/modelers need a demo reel and, for many positions, it's more important than a résumé. In general, the reel should be no longer than two minutes and feature your most amazing content. Put your best work first because you want to make your best impression right away.

A good rule of thumb: if you don't think it's great, don't include it. Animators can present their reel via a link on YouTube or Vimeo. These are the top services for posting videos and films. YouTube may have a bigger audience and get more views, but Vimeo has a feature that allows the user to replace content under the same URL. This can be handy when updating a demo reel. Pixar suggests leaving any music or soundtrack off because it can often be distracting.

A demo reel also needs frames before each sequence of work, telling the background on the piece. Pixar gives this example: "*Sleeping ball: (June 2003) Group project; I shaded the plastic sphere in Slim/Renderman.*" Be sure to say what animation software you used to create the work.

Include a title card at the beginning and end with your name, address, phone, and email. It's often good to show the stages of production—the rigging, the coloring, the shading, and the lighting, for example. Show your reel to others to critique it, and make improvements until it is absolutely polished. You want to present the best sampling of your work possible.

Other standard job-hunting tools include the cover letter. This is the letter you send to an employer along with your résumé that helps explain why you are applying for the job and why you are an ideal candidate. It's a quick sales pitch for yourself. Select people who can be your references. When employers are impressed by a candidate's résumé and cover letter, they often take the next step and call previous employers who can discuss your work history, strengths, and weaknesses. Some employers check references before a personal interview, and some check them afterward.

When an employer calls you in for an interview, you know you are a contender. Making a good impression in person is crucial. Be prepared by practicing your interview skills. Be on time,

The primary tool for any job hunter is the résumé. An impressive one highlights skills, career goals, work experiences, and education. Plus, it should be error-free.

and always follow up by sending a thank-you note. When you do meet with human resources and other staff members of a potential employer, make sure you are dressed correctly. It's often worth the investment to look sharp and dress in such a way that matches the work environment.

Anytime that you're looking for work in this field, make sure you're up-to-date on the latest trends and tools. This is a job where an ongoing education is necessary to advance.

Chapter FIVE

The Cutting-Edge World of 3D

As mentioned in the introduction, 3D animation is entering new worlds. Advances in virtual reality (VR) have opened up a new universe for animators. Through VR, viewers not only feel immersed in 3D animated films, but they are also able to play 3D games that make them feel like they are in the game itself.

"Virtual reality" is a term used to describe a 3D computer-generated environment. Some people already consider some worlds made with 3D animation to be virtual reality. But today, with the use of special goggles or headsets (called head-mounted displays), audiences can completely immerse themselves in a 3D world. Some VR systems come equipped with gloves so the viewer can reach out in a VR world and interact with objects.

The quality of virtual reality has increased in recent years. One of the biggest leaps forward came from the young technology whiz Palmer Luckey. As a teenager, Luckey became obsessed with building his own virtual reality headset. In 2012, at age twenty, he dropped out of college and dedicated himself to the project. The

Virtual reality technology is opening up new worlds for 3D animation. Microsoft's HoloLens, for example, creates holographic images in front of the wearer.

end result was called Oculus Rift, and the technology improved on all VR systems that had come before. The results were so astounding that Mark Zuckerberg, the founder of Facebook, bought Luckey's newly formed VR company for $2 billion in 2014. Other companies have jumped on the VR bandwagon, introducing gear such as the Microsoft HoloLens, Sony's Project Morpheus, The Vive by Valve, and Samsung Gear VR.

Oculus Rift headsets have been adapted for use in games such as *Skyrim.* The game *Elite Dangerous* has a VR version that lets players explore detailed simulated planet surfaces.

These include settlements, space ports, and wrecks, both from a spaceship and from the expansive bubble canopy of the "Scarab" Surface Recon Vehicle (SRV). Real-time rendering is essential to make these interactive computer graphics work. Computers have to create synthetic images fast enough so that the viewer can interact in a virtual environment.

STEPPING INTO A FILM

VR movies are also being made where viewers feel like they are standing in the middle of the action. They can simply turn their heads and get a new view of the filmed events.

On a regular screen, the point of view remains constant, but with VR it can change with every turn of the head. The *Wall Street Journal* recently published an article titled "Virtual Reality: Get Ready for the VR Revolution." The writer said that a VR film might give you the capability to run alongside a character and look over your shoulder to see what's chasing you. A character might point behind you. When you turn around wearing a VR headset, you actually see an approaching monster. You can be at a dinner party, sit at the table, and turn and face whoever is talking.

Oculus Story Studio, a team of film and game developers dedicated to exploring "immersive cinema" for Oculus Rift, has developed a short 3D animated film for children about a hedgehog named Henry. Viewers can look around Henry's home and feel like they are sitting down with him, looking directly into his eyes from across the table. They are developing a film that makes your feel like you are in the ring with a matador and a bull. They want to show that virtual reality is an art form. Watching the Oculus Story Studio movie titled *Lost*, the viewer feels as if he or she is standing in the middle of the woods.

By wearing a VR headset, viewers can be totally immersed in a 3D world and feel as if they are interacting with 3D characters and objects.

When you hear a rustling in the brush to the left, you can turn to see a robot arm moving.

Sony's PlayStation team partnered with Motional, a VR creative company, to produce an interactive VR movie called *Gary the Gull*. Gary responds to actions from the viewer. For example, if you lean in close to him, he will jump back. In time, an interactive glove might let you touch and effect items in the movie. Narrative VR is still just beginning, but it shows a whole new way that 3D animation may be used.

Outside of the entertainment world, 3D virtual reality can have practical applications. For example, pilots can train in simulators that realistically reconstruct what their flights will be like.

3D models and animations are necessary to populate 3D worlds. Yantram Animation Studio has been realizing the practical application of 3D technology and VR. The company is developing applications for the real estate industry that would allow home buyers to virtually walk through homes from any location by strapping on a VR headset. When perfected, the technology should allow users the ability to sit on the furniture, move into any part of the home, and look out windows.

Insight from the Experts

Here is some advice from pros in 3D animation and modeling:

"To be successful in this field, you need to become a problem solver with good observation skills and a desire to create things. You never stop learning in this field. You face new challenges with every new project, many of which require innovative solutions that you must discover on your own." William Vaughan, author of *Digital Modeling*.

"Let's face it: animation is an acting profession. It's important to have some life experience to imbue your characters with. Travel, go to see shows, watch people, write down your ideas, and record memorable moments. In order to animate well, you need to be a great observer."— Andrew Gordon and Robb Denovan, Pixar animators, in an interview in *3D World* magazine.

"Love what you are doing because it [isn't] easy. Once you get out of school, you will get a second education by working in the industry, and your career may take twists and turns you never expected (for the good and bad). Get your foot in the door, grab an internship, make contacts, do good work, go where the work is, build a reel, and a reputation."— Gabriel Polonsky, Gabriel Polonsky Studio, a leading animation company in Boston in *Animation Career Review*, January 12, 2012

Three-dimensional models in virtual reality environments are being developed to train and educate in the fields of medicine, aviation, and military. The technology can be used to make simulated cockpits, operating rooms, and battle conditions. Surgeons, for example, can practice operations with virtual instruments on virtual organs.

In the future, scientists envision customers shopping in virtual stores where they can walk through and view 3D models of actual products and purchase them online. The 3D virtual models can be viewed online as well.

Second Life, an online virtual world, developed by Linden Lab, created an entire 3D world that users can access via the internet. This is a virtual world where people meet, play, go to clubs, and just hang out. They buy land and build homes. Now with Oculus Rift, players can feel like they are actually interacting with the Second Life world.

3D SCANNING AND PRINTING

In recent years, three-dimensional printing has become very popular, and the cost to own a personal 3D printer can be as little as a few hundred dollars. These printers build physical objects by printing layers of material in succession. The objects are built with multiple layers of resin, plaster, metal, or other material.

To create the object, the printer follows a design from a 3D model. Often, 3D models are made from special 3D laser scanners that capture details about an object and computerize them. A 3D artist can create a character from scratch using 3D software, such as Maya, and then print out a real-life model.

People are now using 3D printers to make almost anything—jewelry, housewares, figurines, toys, bird feeders, prosthetic limbs, car parts, utensils, games, and more.

Are you ready to embrace new 3D worlds? With its rapid advances and unique combination of art and technology, 3D animation offers a rewarding and exciting career path.

Advances in scanning technology have helped bring more realistic 3D animations to films and games. For example, with high-tech 360-degree scanning and high-end cameras, a very detailed digital version of a person can be made to create a 3D model. So if making a football video game, for example, a technician could scan the exact features of a player to make a more realistic 3D animated version for the game.

In the film industry, 3D printing is being used to help create physical objects. For example, in the movie *Iron Man 2*, Robert

Downey Jr., wears a suit that was first digitally modeled and then produced in pieces on a 3D printer.

Creators of 3D stop-motion films are also finding big benefits in 3D printing. 3D printing has aided several stop-motion animation film productions—such as the movies *Coraline* and *Paranorman*—by allowing them to easily create multiple faces and props. Producing each frame in stop-motion is extremely laborious. Creating facial expressions alone can be very time-consuming, but when you can design and then easily "print" hundreds of 3D faces, the process becomes very easy.

The world of 3D is rapidly growing, and the possibilities seem almost endless. For example, Google recently introduced Tilt Brush, an extraordinary app for the virtual reality headset HTC Vive. Immersed in darkness and using the specially designed game controllers, users can create 3D art before their eyes. The room becomes a canvas, and the 3D artists can step around and through their drawings as they go. Some of the "materials" for creating are surreal, including virtual fire, stars, and snowflakes.

Although the 3D universe is expanding, it's also getting smaller. Many see that more 3D content will be made available specifically for mobile devices in the future. The new possibilities from 3D modeling and animation are exciting. Innovations and technological advances are making this one of the most enriching, creative, and dynamic career fields on the planet.

Glossary

avar Short for animation variable, which controls the position of part of an animated object. Every part of the model that needs to move is assigned an avar.

CGI (computer-generated imagery) The application of 3D computer graphics to create or contribute to images.

compositing Combining visual elements from separate sources into one frame.

digital Describing electronic technology that creates, stores, and processes data in terms of two states: positive and non-positive. Computers are digital machines because basically they function by distinguishing between just two values, 0 and 1, or off and on.

inbetweening Creating the drawings in between the keyframes in animation.

keyframing Creating several main, distinct frames to represent a single motion.

mesh A 3D representation consisting of polygons and vertices.

motion capture (mocap) A method to digitally record human movement using special sensors. The recorded motion capture data of an actor is applied to a 3D character so it moves naturally as the actor does.

pixel From the words "picture element," an individual dot from an image on a computer screen.

polycount The total number of polygons in a 3D model.

polygon Any two-dimensional shape with straight sides.

postproduction Work done on a film or video game after the recording of the primary content has taken place.

preproduction The planning stage; work done on a film, TV show, or video game before content starts being produced.

rendering The process of making an image based on three-dimensional data stored within a computer.

rigging A digital skeleton bound to a 3D mesh. The rigging will have a set of animation controls so the animator can manipulate the figure.

skin The covering that is projected over the mesh.

stop-motion A method to animate figures by stopping and starting the camera and incrementally moving the figures.

texture mapping The equivalent of applying wrapping paper or paint to an object but with a computerized 3D model. The mapping gives the 3D model a surface texture.

vertex Each angular point of a polygon or other figure.

virtual reality An immersive, computer-simulated environment that seems like a real environment.

For More Information

The Animation Guild
1105 N. Hollywood Way
Burbank, CA 91505
(818) 845-7500
Website: www.animationguild.org

This members' guild of animators provides news affecting
those in the animation industry.

Blender Foundation
Entrepotdok 57A 1018 AD
Amsterdam
the Netherlands
Email: foundation@blender.org
Website: https://www.blender.org

The Blender Foundation is a Dutch public-benefit corporation
that, in part, supports its free and open-source 3D creation
suite.

Canadian Advanced Technology Alliance (CATA)
207 Bank Street, Suite 416
Ottawa, ON K2P 2N2
(613) 236-6550
Website: www.cata.ca

The largest high-tech association in Canada, CATA is a
comprehensive resource, providing the latest high-tech
news in Canada.

Canadian Association for Computer Science
5090 Explorer Drive, Suite 801
Mississauga, ON L4W 4T9
(905) 602-1370
Website: www.cips.ca

Information is provided here for those pursuing or advancing a
career in computer science or software engineering.

Information Technology Association of Canada
220 Laurier Avenue West, Suite 1120
Ottawa, ON K1P 5Z9
(613) 238-4822
Website: www.itac.ca

This organization focuses on business issues related to
information technology in Canada. The site features news
for professionals about computer software and electronic
services.

Institute of Electrical and Electronics Engineers/Computer
Society
2001 L Street NW, Suite 700
Washington, DC 20036-4928
(202) 371-0101
Website: www.computer.org

The world's leading membership organization dedicated to
computer science and technology offers information,
networking, and career-development resources.

Women in Animation
c/o Perry, Neidorf & Grassl, LLP
Attn: Marine Hekimian
11400 W. Olympic Boulevard, # 590
Los Angeles, CA 90064
Website: www.womeninanimation.org

This institution brings together women to share resources, advice, and opportunities.

WEBSITES

Because of the changing nature of internet links, Rosen Publishing has developed an online list of websites related to the subject of this book. This site is updated regularly. Please use this link to access the list:

http://www.rosenlinks.com/TTHIC/3D

For Further Reading

Amin, Jahirul. *Beginner's Guide to Character Creation in Maya.* Worcestershire, UK: 3D Total Printing, 2015.

Beane, Andy. *3D Animation Essentials.* Hoboken, NJ: Sybex/Wiley, 2012.

Blazer, Liz. *Animated Storytelling: Simple Steps for Creating Animation and Motion Graphics.* Berkeley, CA: Peachpit Press/Pearson Education, 2015.

Catmull, Ed. *Creativity, Inc.: Overcoming the Unseen Forces That Stand in the Way of True Inspiration.* New York, NY: Random House, 2014.

Cavalier, Stephen. *The World History of Animation.* Berkeley, CA: University of California Press, 2011.

Chandler, Matt. *3ds Max Projects: A Detailed Guide to Modeling, Texturing, Rigging, Animation and Lighting.* Worcestershire, UK: 3D Total Printing, 2014.

Chopine, Ami. *3D Art Essentials: The Fundamentals of 3D Modeling, Texturing, and Animation.* Oxfordshire, UK: Focal Press, 2011.

Davis, Bradley, Austin Karen Bryla, and Phillips Alexander Benton. *Oculus Rift in Action.* Greenwich, CT: Manning Publications, 2014.

Eaton, Tristan. *The 3D Art Book.* New York, NY: Prestel, 2011.

Henry, Kevin. *Drawing for Product Designers.* London, UK: Laurence King Publishing, 2012.

Lord, Peter. *Cracking Animation: The Aardman Book of 3-D Animation,* 3rd ed. London, UK: Thames & Hudson, 2010.

Mullen, Tony. *Introducing Character Animation with Blender.* Hoboken, NJ: Sybex/Wiley, 2011.

Nite, Sky. *Virtual Reality Insider: Guidebook for the VR Industry.* Swansea, UK: New Dimension Entertainment, 2014.

Rogers, Scott. *Level Up! The Guide to Great Video Game Design.* Hoboken, NJ: Wiley, 2014.

Roy, Kenny. *How to Cheat in Maya 2014: Tools and Techniques for Character Animation.* Oxfordshire, UK: Focal Press, 2011.

Thilakanathan, Danan. *3D Modeling for Beginners: Learn Everything You Need to Know About 3D Modeling!* Seattle. WA: Amazon Digital Services, 2016.

Vaughan, William. *Digital Modeling.* Berkeley, CA: New Riders, 2012.

Villar, Oliver. *Learning Blender: A Hands-On Guide to Creating 3D Animated Characters.* Upper Saddle River, NJ: Addison-Wesley/Pearson Education, 2015.

Williams, Richard. *The Animator's Survival Kit.* London, UK: Faber & Faber, 2002.

"Animate Like a Pixar Pro." CreativeBloq, September 12, 2013. Retrieved May 7, 2016. http://www.creativebloq.com/ animation/animate-pixar-pro-9134381.

"Animated Films." AMC Filmsite. Retrieved May 7, 2016. http:// www.filmsite.org/animatedfilms.html.

"Computer Animation: How to Be a Computer Animator." Study.com. Retrieved May 7, 2016. http://study.com/ articles/Computer_Animation_How_to_Be_a_Computer_ Animator.html.

Cox, Tom. "The Incredible Technology That Changed the Face of Animation." Moviepilot, March 11, 2016. http://moviepilot. com/posts/3815513.

"Creating an Animation Demo Reel – The Complete Guide." Bloop Animation. Retrieved May 7, 2016. https://www. bloopanimation.com/animation-demo-reel.

"Fancy Names & Fun Toys: Praxinoscope." Museum of the History of Science. Retrieved May 7, 2016. http://www.mhs. ox.ac.uk/exhibits/fancy-names-and-fun-toys/praxinoscope.

Fronczak, Tom. "10 Types of 3D Animation Software Worth Knowing." *Animation Career Review*, May 10, 2011. http:// www.animationcareerreview.com/ articles/10-types-3d-animation-software-worth-knowing.

Hegg, Robin. "The Art of Programming in Computer Animation." IEEESpark, December 2014. http://spark.ieee. org/2014-issue-4/ the-art-of-programming-in-computer-animation.

"Highest box office film gross for an animation—inflation adjusted." Guinness World Records. Retrieved May 7, 2016. http://www.guinnessworldrecords.com/world-records/highest-box-office-film-gross-for-an-animation-inflation-adjusted.

"History of 3D Animation." Animation Academy. Retrieved May 7, 2016. http://multimediamcc.com/old-students/ashaver/3d_history.html.

Holmes, Stephen. "The Evolution of CG Software." 3D Artist. Retrieved May 7, 2016. http://www.3dartistonline.com/news/2013/12/the-evolution-of-cg-software.

"How to Get a Job at Pixar Studios." CreativeBloq, October 25, 2012. http://www.creativebloq.com/animation/job-at-pixar-10121018.

Kazmeyer, Milton. "The Art and Science of Computer Animation." Chron. Retrieved May 7, 2016. http://smallbusiness.chron.com/art-science-computer-animation-37935.html.

Mitchell, Kate. "Could VR Transform the World of 3D Animation?" Leap Motion, May 2, 2015. http://blog.leapmotion.com/vr-transform-world-3d-animation.

Schwartzel, Erich. "Virtual Reality: Get Ready for the VR Revolution." *Wall Street Journal*, March 4, 2016. http://www.wsj.com/articles/virtual-reality-movies-get-ready-for-the-vr-revolution-1457030357.

Silverman, David. "3D Primer for Game Developers: An Overview of 3D Modeling in Games." Envatotuts+, March 5, 2013. http://gamedevelopment.tutsplus.com.

Takahashi, Dean. "How Pixar Made *Monsters University*, Its Latest Technological Marvel." VentureBeat.com, April 24, 2013. http://venturebeat.com/2013/04/24/the-making-of-pixars-latest-technological-marvel-monsters-university.

"3D Scanning for Video Games." Graphine, December 18, 2014. Retrieved May 7, 2016. http://graphinesoftware.com/blog/2014-12-18-3d-scanning-for-video-games.

VRHunter. "What Filmmakers, Storytellers and Games Devs Are Saying About the Future of VR." VRCircle, January 21, 2016. http://www.vrcircle.com/post/What-filmmakers-storytellers-and-games-devs-are-saying-about-the-future-of-VR.

Wilding, Robin. "Tangible Advice from the Pros for Future Animators." *Animation Career Review*, February 28, 2012. http://www.animationcareerreview.com/articles/tangible-advice-pros-future-animators.

ABOUT THE AUTHOR

Don Rauf is the author of more than thirty nonfiction books, including *Killer Lipstick and Other Spy Gadgets*, *American Inventions*, *Virtual Reality*, *Getting the Most Out of Makerspaces to Explore Arduino & Electronics*, *Getting the Most Out of Makerspaces to Build Unmanned Aerial Vehicles*, and *Powering Up a Career in Internet Security*.

PHOTO CREDITS

Cover © iStockphoto.com/vgajic; p. 5 South_Agency/E+/Getty Images; p. 8 UpperCut Images/Getty Images; p. 9 Science & Society Picture Library/Getty Images; p. 11 Ronald Grant Archive/Alamy Stock Photo; pp. 14–15 © Pixar Animation Studios/Courtesy: Everett Collection; pp. 17, 64 AF archive/Alamy Stock Photo; pp. 19, 21 Hill Street Studios/Blend Images/Getty Images; p. 23 Photofusion/Universal Images Group/Getty Images; pp. 25, 60 © AP Images; p. 28 Richard Cummins/Lonely Planet Images/Getty Images; p. 31 Pasieka/Science Photo Library/Getty Images; p. 33 Moviestore Collection Ltd/Alamy Stock Photo; p. 35 ZUMA Press, Inc./Alamy Stock Photo; p. 36 Pictorial Press Ltd/Alamy Stock Photo; p. 41 Phil Rees/REX/Newscom; p. 44 © dpa picture alliance/Alamy Stock Photo; pp. 46, 48–49 Bloomberg/Getty Images; p. 52 © IanDagnall Computing/Alamy Stock Photo; pp. 54–55 Steve Debenport/E+/Getty Images; p. 58 Microsoft/REX/AP Images; p. 61 Fabrice Coffrini/AFP/Getty Images; back cover and interior pages background image Vladgrin/Shutterstock.com.

Designer: Nicole Russo; Editor: Nicholas Croce;
Photo Researcher: Nicole Baker